DINGUS GUY

Intense Romance Erotica

THE NEXT
Customer
GUARD DON OF EDEN

WARNING

This book contains sexually explicit scenes and adult language. It may be considered offensive to some readers. This book is for sale to adults ONLY.

* * * * * * * * * * * * * * * * * * *

Please store your files wisely where they cannot be accessed by underage readers.

Please feel free to send me an email. Just know that these emails are filtered by my publisher. Good news is always welcome.

Dingus Guy - **dingus_guy@awesomeauthors.org**

You might also want to check my blog for Updates and interesting info. http://dingus-guy.awesomeauthors.org/

About the Publisher

4Fun Publishing, a member of **BLVNP Incorporated**, 340 S. Lemon #6200, Walnut CA 91789, info@blvnp.com / legal@blvnp.com
NOTE: Due to the highly emotional reaction of some people to works of erotic fiction, any email sent to the above address that contains foul language or religious references is automatically deleted by our anti-spam software and will not be seen. All other communications are welcome.

DISCLAIMER

Please don't be stupid and kill yourself. This book is a work of FICTION. Do not try any new sexual practice that you find in this book. It is fiction and not to be confused with reality. Neither the author nor the publisher or its associates assume any responsibility for any loss, injury, death or legal consequences resulting from acting on the contents in this book. Every character in this book is over 18 years of age. The author's opinions are not to be construed as the opinions of the publisher. The material in this book is for entertainment purposes ONLY. Enjoy.

The Next Customer
Guard Don of Eden
Intense Romance Erotica

By: Dingus Guy

ISBN: 978-1-68030-510-4

"Those who believe that destiny is the prime mover of all things say: We should not exert ourselves to acquire wealth, for sometimes it is not acquired although we strive to get it, while at other times it comes to us of itself without any exertion on our part. Everything is therefore in the power of destiny, who is the lord of gain and loss, of success and defeat, of pleasure and pain."

- Kama Sutra

Chapter 1

Eden Spa and Resort was a place to come when spirits were low. When stress was too much in one's life. You came to unwind and let loose all inhibitions. Massages were recommended, drinks were served and the exotic backdrop was enticing. You came to find yourself and sometimes found another. Couples came to reinvigorate their relationships. Others came to explore. Love was always in the air. You could hear it, see it, and often smell it. When it was your turn, you would experience it.

Don had come to Eden to work, with no other intentions. He was hired to run security and had several fine references to help him acquire the position. The place ran itself, but when alcohol did its tricks, no one could predict the outcome. He was needed more at night than during the day, but the days were not problem-free. He just didn't have to worry about anything while the sun was up.

As soon as the sun set, Don was on call until sunrise. He generally worked 7PM-3AM, but occasionally was called to help with unruly guests. At 225 lbs, 6'5" he had the most intimidating stance. Folded arms, a piercing stare, and a deep voice was usually enough to stop most altercations. He rarely had to get involved. He had a 3-inch scar on his left cheek right below one of his emerald eyes. He was lucky not to have been blinded, but it was the only time anyone had wounded him. It was this wound more than any of his facial features that made him a man not to be trifled with. It was his badge of courage.

In stepped Autumn Hunt. All 5' 8", 119 lbs of tanned blonde exquisite beauty that Don took for another average vacationer. He was not against having sex with the clientele. He just didn't do it. When he first met her, she was singing karaoke in the lounge. She didn't exactly have the pipes of a songbird, but her rendition of "Frosty the Snowman" brought down the house. She sang it in such a sexy voice and presented it in a very comical way that all eyes were on her.

Don watched her sing and ignored the potential drunkard at the bar. She wore a teal and pink sarong around her hips, covering her waist and most of her right leg. Her left leg was silky and smooth and glistened in the lights of the stage area. Her top was just a pink lycra string bikini. Her golden hair was tied in a ponytail by a pink silk ribbon. Her puffy pink glossy lips wrapped around her pearly white smile. Her blue eyes made contact with all of her audience. It was as if her smile and her eyes were one. If you met her gaze, you were touched by her smile that you would swear was meant only for you. The crowd clapped loudly and she went back to her stool and raised her umbrella drink in appreciation to her adoring fans. The drunkard at the bar was getting a little bit sloppy and reached out to grab at the young lady. She slapped his hand away and he flipped some peanuts from the bar at her. Don was immediately on top of the man and before anything else could go wrong he muscled him out of the bar. He told one of his men to make sure he was escorted back to his bungalow. When he returned the young lady was gone.

It was about 11am the next morning when Don walked along the pool area to take in his daily plunge into the jacuzzi. He was happy to see the lack of bodies poolside. At this time the spa organized a mountain hike that was due back a little before noon for lunch. As Don relaxed in the warm bubbling water, a woman with a white string bikini entered the picture opposite of Don. Her shadow fell across Don and he was alerted to her presence. He failed to realize it was the woman from the previous nights festivities until she introduced herself.

"Thanks for the help last night," Autumn announced. Don opened his eyes and met her teeth and eye combo. She was enchanting. The hair was no longer in a ponytail instead hung straight back to the midway point of her back. There was no sarong to cover her legs and hips. Her attire was a surprising one piece white bathing suit. Her curves were accentuated and her breasts pushed forward quite well. Her legs were tanned and shapely. He didn't want to be rude and stare, so he held up his hand to shield the sun behind her and this helped to also shield his wandering eyes.

"Just doing my job ma'am," Don responded with a wild west styled demeanor.

"My name is Autumn, not ma'am," she demanded. She waved her hand towards the jacuzzi, in a gesture to gather if it was acceptable to join him. He reciprocated the hand movement with one of his own.

"Sorry force of habit," Don apologized. "My name is Don."

"Glad to meet you Don," Autumn returned, as she stepped into the jacuzzi hand extended. He politely grabbed it and the greeting was delivered. Her infectious smile charming the smile right out of the corners of his mouth.

"Likewise, Autumn."

"I noticed a bit of a New York accent there Don," Autumn guessed.

"Indeed," Don replied, "I am a born and raised Long Island boy."

"I have family there on the eastern end. They love fishing."

"Fishing is big there," Don agreed. "I never really got into it, I was too busy playing ball with my neighborhood buddies."

"So what brings you all the way out to Eden? Is it the island that makes you feel like you are back home?"

"Long Island might be an island, but it far from Eden. Besides who would not want a job here?" Don retorted.

"Answers a question with a question," Autumn smirked.

"Here is another one. What brings you here?"

"Plenty of reasons actually. For starters, I am looking for a fun time of course," she replied. "Eden was recommended by a friend. She told me it was the place to go to get away from life's headaches. She showed me the catalog and I was sold. I loved the vigorous exercise classes and different levels of hiking. I am an exercise nut. Then there were all these classes about meditation, Pilates, yoga and they were all outside. Even the massages were outside. I love that aspect. Fresh air and sunshine."

"You came to the right place for that," Don added. "Many people come here to escape. Some come to start over, some come to party and just forget. Others just want to relax. Eden has a lot of enticing things."

"I can see that," Autumn stated, obviously by the turn of her head, flirting with Don. Don felt life beneath his swim trunks as her eyes held his gaze. Don was not one to look away so he stared back.

Eager to change the subject, Don took the initiative. "Have you had time to work out your headaches with a massage yet?"

"Oh yes," Autumn exclaimed, "I had the most amazing massage with these little warm stones..."

"The hot stone treatment," Don interjected.

"Exactly! Don, I don't know what those people get paid, but it isn't nearly enough. I was so relaxed, I fell asleep on the table. That has never happened before."

"I have had the hot stone treatment on more than one occasion, and I have fallen asleep with each one."

"Ah the fringe benefits of the job," Autumn declared.

"It does have its many advantages," Don answered. He extended his arms wide around the jacuzzi like the king of his castle and grinned.

"I will assume you were talking about me," Autumn teased. Thank you Don."

Don immediately became tongue-tied and fumbled for a response. She caught sight of his awkwardness and pounced.

"Wow," Autumn began, "look at the tough security man turn red." She giggled playfully. Don snickered and splashed some water towards Autumn with the back of his hand. "Oh, no you didn't!"

"I do believe I did," Don smirked.

Before he could even try to stop her, she darted forward. Immersing herself in the water head first, she grabbed his legs and with a quick tug Don slid under. She let go as soon as the momentum carried him into the water. The entire attack took no more than 3 seconds to pull off and another 5 to prop herself back to where she started. Don floundered a little to regain his balance and emerged looking surprised and unsure of his next move. Wiping his eyes clear of water he gazed over at the smiling blonde who clearly looked overjoyed at what she had accomplished. She was clearly a lot stronger than she looked, he thought.

"I hope I didn't embarrass you Don," Autumn apologized with no clear indication on her face that she meant what she just said. She was a big flirt, Don thought.

"I don't embarrass easily," Don answered, pausing for effect and then added, "but I do get even."

"Now you sound like a movie cliché."

"Sooo," Don returned, "what do you do back in the real world?"

"Ha," Autumn mused, "look at you changing the subject. Okay, well I work with lifeguards and the safety aspect of their job. Introducing new products to improve their work environment. We have taken steps to convert most of the personnel recreational areas in beaches across Southern California to solar power to help save money and help the environment. Most of the supplies, whether it be Band-Aids, life vests, lifeguard swim gear all are made from organic materials. Many of the lifeguards have recognized a need for change, and it is my job to help sell this idea and push our products."

"Sounds interesting. Do you enjoy it?"

"Hell yeah," Autumn agreed, "It's not every day that you work a few hours and then lie out on beaches working on your tan."

"Sounds like my job," Don laughed.

"Well, I don't have to beat anyone up."

"I think you have the wrong impression of me," Don declared. "I rarely have to get physical with anyone."

"I am sure you just have to stand over them, and your shadow does the work."

"Pretty much. It helps to be big and scary looking."

"Sexy too," Autumn added. Don rolled his eyes and she smiled again. "You might be all beefy with big muscles, tall and wide shouldered and can stare smaller people down with those sparkling emerald eyes, but you know you are extremely handsome. Don't even try and deny it."

"I appreciate the compliments, so far be it from me to deny such a beautiful lady."

"Awww, how sweet," Autumn said. "You are a real charmer. Now the big question, do you have a girl?"

"I have little time to give to a relationship, so no."

"I didn't ask about a relationship, I was just inquiring whether or not you would be free for a little of my company if I pursued it."

"You are quite direct Autumn," Don countered.

"It doesn't hurt to be direct when you see someone you would like to get to know."

"I suppose it doesn't. I guess I am not used to being hit on so hard."

"I don't believe that," Autumn challenged. "I am sure plenty of girls have tried to come on to you."

"Well," Don responded, "perhaps not in the same fashion. Every night, I get looks, but I can't let my guard down. Some bungalow numbers have been given to me, some pinching and groping have been attempted, but when I am on duty, I am on duty."

"What about times like now? You aren't working now are you?"

"No, I am not working, but usually I keep to myself. Most of the guests are doing our hikes at this hour, so I can lounge with little to no interruption."

"Am I interrupting?" Autumn questioned.

"Sorry," Don apologized, "I did not mean to imply that at all. You are a welcome distraction to my daily Jacuzzi fix."

"Are you sure, because I can certainly leave as fast as I pulled you under water?" Autumn smirked. Don couldn't help be overcome by her womanly charms. He was a man after all, and it had been quite a few months since he was with a woman. He was intrigued to say the least.

"I am fine," Don admitted.

"So Don, are you interested in my advances?" Autumn inquired.

"I have never had any intimate relations with a guest before, and to be truthful with you Autumn, I am not sure what is to gained from it."

"I admire that Don," Autumn praised, "but let me ask you this. If I wasn't a guest, but someone you met at a casual function or something of the like, would you be more likely to be interested?"

"It probably would be easier, yes."

"Okay, so if you have some interest. Let us stop there. You are not working until when?"

"My hours are steady from 7pm until the early hours of the morning."

"Would you come to a class with me?" Autumn proposed.

"A class?" Don asked.

"There goes that answering a question with a question thing again. Yes, a class. One of the many Eden classes. I am not inviting you back to my bungalo for a cup of coffee or a glass of wine. Just a class."

"I am intrigued, which class?"

"Well," Autumn began, "I thought you would choose one that maybe you never tried before, but were always interested in trying."

"Wouldn't you rather choose one?"

"No," Autumn started. "The way I see it, if we have fun at a class you chose, then I can choose the next one and we can do it again. What do you think? Up for a class?"

"I am not promising anything more though," Don said.

"I am not asking for anything more," Autumn replied. "Just pick a class, we meet there, see how it goes."

"Okay, sure," Don agreed. Her smile was so infectious. Any regret he might have felt in making such a decision had suddenly melted away. "I will have to look over the schedule first, and see how it fits."

"That is fine with me. I am very happy you said yes. I am going to take a shower get dressed and go to Tranquility Cove for some lunch. Meet me there around one o'clock and we can discuss the class you picked."

"Sounds good," Don answered. As Autumn stood up out of the water, Don rose as well. He suddenly realized something and must have gave off an usual face because Autumn saw it. She smiled, understanding what he must have been thinking.

"Yes?" Autumn asked innocently.

"You just tricked me into lunch, didn't you?"

"Are you going to meet me at 1pm for lunch?"

"I suppose so," Don affirmed.

"Then, yes, I tricked you," Autumn responded gleefully. She turned and giggled as she walked away.

Chapter 2

Don caught Autumn right away as soon as he walked through the door. She once again had her hair in a ponytail. Her clothes were not as revealing as the last two times he had seen her. She wore a black leotard, tight against her body, hiding her beautiful legs. Obviously dressed for the class, she thought Don would eventually choose. She would have to change.

"Hey again," Autumn greeted.

"I hope I didn't keep you long," Don asked.

"No," Autumn replied, "I just sat down three minutes before you got here."

"That's a relief. Wouldn't want to make a pretty lady wait."

"Wow that is corny," Autumn laughed giving Don a wink of approval.

"Sometimes corny works."

"It often does, I will admit. Nothing like a guy who holds the car door open for a woman. I laugh each time, because it is so chauvinistic."

"How so?" Don questioned.

"Well there are certain things in life that a man has adopted as things to do for the woman. They get this gentlemen tag like a badge of courage. If we do something for the man in our lives, we are called good housekeepers."

"That isn't always true," Don retorted.

"You would be hard pressed to find an occurrence where the woman holds the door for the guy, because it isn't an accepted practice. Be right back I have to use the bathroom." As she rose to leave, Don stood up. She sat down looked at Don and smiled as he looked down at her with a questionable look on his face.

"Like standing up at a restaurant," Autumn continued. "A woman never stands up for a guy, it isn't in the rule book."

"You are a something else Autumn."

"Thank you Don."

They ordered and ate food, talked about life inside and outside the resort, and dating. When it was time to announce the class, Don smiled and told her she would have to change back into a bathing suit in order to participate.

"Is it going to be a surprise or are you going to tell me?" Autumn asked.

"It is a surprise. You see I figured you might have all ready looked over the schedule of classes and figured what I might choose. So I pulled a favor from a co-worker and got a class not on the schedule."

"Oh nice, very resourceful."

"I try, but for now go and get changed and meet me in the Casa Spa Room at the Serenity Building in 15 minutes. You know where that is?"

"I very much do. I can't wait."

"See you in a little bit then."

When Autumn opened the door to the Casa Spa room, she was shocked to see a large mat and in the center were towels and a lounge chair. Don was situated in the lounge chair with his arms folded behind his head. He was wearing no top and a pair of Hawaiian boxer trunks. His chest was rippled with muscles and the tan was practically perfectly bronzed. She had taken notice of this in the Jacuzzi, but never really got a good look until now, because of the water. A dark-skinned woman stood right behind him shaking a bottle of liquid.

"What have we here?" Autumn inquired. She looked around for another lounge chair and found none.

"This is Hullimanda, and I will let her explain the class," Don returned.

"Hello Autumn," Hullimanda spoke with the thickest of island accents. It might have been Jamaican, but she wasn't sure. "Welcome to my class, Accu-Massage."

"Ha," Autumn hooted. "You will learn the basics of the pressure points located on and around the foot. You will find out how to give a fantastic massage while receiving one in return. The foot is filled with many pressure areas that can relieve pain throughout the body. You will use these points of interest for yourself and others."

Hullimanda handed Autumn the bottle she had been shaking and told her to kneel in front of Don and prepare to begin the lesson. She looked over at Don. He was smiling from ear to ear.

"I figure," Don announced, "I would go first because I wouldn't want to disappoint you with the old standby, lady's first routine. I know how you feel about that."

"Smart ass," Autumn declared. She knelt down in front of Don and he thrust a barefoot at her. She smacked it playfully away from her face.

"Now, now woman, you best behave or I will have Hullimanda go right to the toe sucking lesson instead."

"You big brute," Autumn said laughing as she said it. She followed Hullimanda's words, applying the sweet smelling oil on her hands, and onto his toes and glided her hands along his right foot. She applied pressure in certain areas and forced a grimace and a sigh every now and then. She was doing a fine job, and Don let her know it as she proceeded. In time, they switched positions and Don too went to work. Autumn closed her eyes and at one point fell asleep in the chair.

"Wake up sleepy head," Don announced. "You must have enjoyed my work, because you started to snore much like the sound of a hacksaw."

"I was bored," Autumn retorted with a huge grin. "Actually that was very relaxing. I am surprised you would have picked a class like this. I was in store for some heavy duty aerobics class or even some martial arts or something to knock me out another way."

"Well, I always wanted to learn this, but this is a couple's class, so I never had a chance until now."

"Did you have a good time?" Autumn asked.

"Oh yeah," having a girl on her knees in front of me, is always a party." They both laughed.

"So, you interested in another class with me?" Autumn inquired.

"I would love to, your choice of course," Don answered.

"Of course," Autumn agreed. "I have a class in mind that starts at 5pm and is just an hour long, is that too much for you before you start work?"

"I figure you would want to start tomorrow, but I can definitely do another one. Sure." Meet me on the beach at 4:45pm by the Tiki Jungolo, wearing the same outfit or something similar. Okay?"

"Sounds right to me."

Chapter 3

"I will completely understand if you do not wish to go through with this class." Autumn sat with a mango fusion frozen drink explaining herself to Don.

"Why? What is it?"

"It's a Tantric class, fully clothed though and no touching in any intimate way."

"You mean the class that teaches you about prolonged sex without the act of sex?"

"It is a little more than that. Have you ever tried it?"

"No, the truth is, I thought it was a whole lot of mumbo jumbo."

"Will you try it with me?" Autumn asked, batting her eyes and pouting ever so briefly to charm a yes out of him.

"Yes, sure why not. You did say it was fully clothed, right?"

She grabbed the Spa pamphlet from the bar top and flipped to the proper page. She had brought the pamphlet with her to the tiki lounge just in case he wanted more info as was the case.

"The class is called, Touch-free Tantric. It says, explore the intimate life of Tantra and find the secrets of pleasure locked away deep inside of yourself. You will find each breath will bring more erotic fulfillment than the actual sex act itself. Bring light, sexy clothes and a willing partner and enjoy the tantric spirit of another. Nudity is optional."

"Optional?" Don reported.

"It isn't required Don. Like I said, if you do not feel comfortable, please don't feel obligated to do it."

"I will do it, don't worry about it. You have been a pure pleasure to be around all day, and if it takes a little tantra to make you happy, I am all about the tantra."

"Too sweet," Autumn said. "Now we better go or we will be late." She grabbed his hand and pulled him away from his stool towards the beach area. They walked towards a group of people sitting down on various colored blankets on top of the sand. At the far area kneeling on pillows was a guy Don had seen from time to time, but never was introduced to. Their paths never crossed until now. They gave each other a nod of recognition, but little else. He was obviously the instructor, but the turban on his head, made him look like a swami ready to raise snakes out of a basket. Autumn chose an empty are on their own private blankets and waited for the class to start.

As they looked around, most of the other people were paired off, some were partially naked, some were completed naked. There were even some couples of the same sex. This made Don smile. Autumn caught that and inquired with a raised eyebrow.

"I was just thinking," Don whispered.

"Thinking about what?" Autumn quietly asked.

"Well, in this day and age, even the gays were using tantra."

Autumn let out a loud chuckle and snort and she quickly covered her mouth. Don just shrugged his shoulders and smiled at the others looking in their direction.

"Snorting? How lady like," Don chided.

"You bastard," Autumn groaned.

"I am only joking, I like girls that sound like pigs." Autumn reached over and punched him in the arm. Don winced playfully, rubbing his arm as if a painful blow had been thrown at him. The man in the turban interrupted their fun as he introduced himself to the group.

"Thank you all for coming to Touch-free Tantric. My name is Samduri, but you all can call me Sam for short. It is easier to remember." A small chuckle from some of the group. "For those of you not familiar with Tantra, it simply is a way to achieve a higher sexual pleasure through repetition of breathing, our five senses and concentration.

"In Touch-free Tantric, we take what we know about Tantra and remove the elements of physicality. One must not smell a rose to imagine his fragrant scent. One must not hear the sound of traffic in a city to listen to how it is perceived in your mind. One must not be in front of a beautiful sunset to remember what it looks like. One must not taste a piece of sweet fruit to recall the flavor on the tongue. You see the mind is so powerful, and you can store and recall memories as you see fit.

"Now I mentioned 4 of the 5 senses. What about touch? Can you recall the feel of a soft pillow if it isn't in your hand?" Sam held up one of the pillows in front of him. Squeezing it between his hands he continued, "It is far easier to do as I am doing now, but I can put the pillow down and feel it as real as if it was still in my hand. You all have the ability to do the same. Now I know this is touch-free, but for one brief moment touch your partner's cheek with the back and palm of your hand." Don felt Autumn's warm, soft cheek with the back of his hand, and at the same time he felt her touch upon his face. He welcomed the touch with a smile and she returned it. Sam told them to stop and they reluctantly withdrew their hands

"What a simple gesture that was. Take a moment now and remember what that felt like. It happened only seconds ago now. Remember the feel of the other person's cheek. Remember their hand upon yours. Please close your eyes and think about it briefly now."

Trying to recall the softness of Autumn's cheek and hand was easy since it just happened. His mind drifted quickly to her face and mostly to that perfect smile of hers. His train of thought was quickly brought back to the class as Sam continued once more.

"That was pretty easy, right?" Sam asked, as he watched heads nod the affirmation to his question. "That is only a small part of what your mind can do. I want everyone to kneel while facing your partner. Try to go as close to them as you can without touching. It is very important that you achieve this. Closer if you can. Good. Now, I will guide you, but while you listen, you will look directly into each other's eyes. See what they see. See why they came here. See why they chose you to come experience this type of pleasure. There might be all kinds of reasons, but the eyes don't lie. You can see the need for something more there.

"Being so close to each other, you can feel their warmth rise from their body to yours. You thought about their cheek before, but what about their shoulders? Perhaps you are thinking about the muscles in the small of their back now. Think about your partner embracing you. As I walk around to each one of you, I will tap you on the shoulder, at which point you will raise your arms as if you were going to embrace your partner with a warm hug. Your cheek will come as close to your mate as you can get without touching. You will feel their warmth, their closeness, and imagine their arms around you. You will breathe in their scent and hear their breathing too. Breathing is the most important thing in Tantric exercises, so please pay close attention to your own as well. Some people lose focus and actually forget to breathe."

A small murmur of chuckling interrupted Sam, and his smile acknowledged it. "Yes," he continued, "people do forget to exhale. Focusing upon your partner sometimes we lose focus on our own physical being. We have to remember to breathe in and out in a regular pace. You might think how natural that sounds, but it actually takes practice. I guarantee that half you here will have to be reminded by me or your partner to exhale."

Don was startled for a moment as he felt the sudden hand on his shoulder. It was Sam, letting Don know he was to initiate the exercise now, so he leaned in as if he was going to hug Autumn. Their eyes followed each other as their cheeks came to rest within inches away. He did feel her heat, and he did hear her breathing, as he was sure she heard his. He took her scent in, a sweet sexy perfume, that he had noticed before while they were at the Tiki lounge. There was something extremely erotic about what they were doing, tantra or no tantra.

"You are all doing very well," Sam admired. "Now lean back and let your partner try. Remember, do not touch."

Don held still as Autumn leaned into him. He was hoping that she would brush her supple chest into his own, but she held her distance. Instead of going directly cheek to cheek, she brought her mouth close to his as if a kiss was coming. Her eyes locked onto his, and as she licked her lips in temptation, Don felt a gulp rise in his throat as she turned and her breath resounded in his ear. The perfume growing more intensely arousing as her neck went by his nose. He was becoming uncomfortably aroused in his present position and wanted to shift a little to let his hardening cock breath some. He didn't dare be the first one to make contact, so he held strong in his posture.

She came back around from the right cheek, locking eyes once more with Don, each other feeling their warm breaths. Their mouths inches apart, she whispered, "Don?"

"Yes Autumn," Don whispered softly back.

"Is this making you as hot as it is making me?"

"Yes," Don answered quietly. Their eyes held their desire as Autumn moved her face around to his left side and blew lightly in his ear. It sent a chill along his spine. She was getting to him.

"Well done ladies and gentlemen, well done," Sam announced. "Let us now do a new exercise. It is purely optional, but if you would like to be nude, you will find it highly enjoyable. If you do not wish to do so, then it is fine, you will still be able to feel the heightened arousal, but not as strong. I will give you a moment to decide while I pass out pillows to each one of you." Sam reached behind him, where pillows were stacked together and started to distribute one to each couple.

"Is it okay Don if I get undressed?" Autumn inquired softly. She wore an innocent look, but behind those baby blue eyes, Don could feel a wild he had not yet met in any woman before. He very much wanted to see her nakedness, and as much as he tried to be a gentleman, he was realizing that she was pulling him in. As if the lunch wasn't calculated enough, he felt he was manipulated into this class. A part of him knew that at the very least, he would have had to agree to let her choose a class just to be a gentleman. She somehow knew he would. So here he was at a class that was meant to stimulate and titillate, and being asked whether or not it was okay to see a beautiful woman's body. All the while under his shorts his brain had relocated and this question had become the most rhetorical of a question as ever had been asked. He affirmed her wishes with a nod of the head.

"Will you undress with me?" Autumn asked. She undid her bikini top and she let it fall to the blanket. Don couldn't hold his eyes to hers, and she knew he would look. So he did, and when he looked up, her smile wrapped his thumping heart and he smiled back. In most circumstances, he would give her a flat rejection. He was at his place of work and undressing in such a fashion would be a direct violation of most any contract, but he was at Eden. Upper management didn't care what their employees did off the clock and with whom they did it with. As long as no money was exchanged and everything was kept in the up and up, Don was free to do what he wanted. He just had never crossed that line in his years of employment. There were plenty of island women to meet away from Eden, so it wasn't a problem for him. Besides, Don felt obliged to keep it professional because security wasn't a job to show weakness. Yet, as he looked up to Autumn's sparkling eyes again, he relented.

"Yes," Don replied finally. They both looked at each other as they lowered their hands to drop their garments. Don's semi-erect penis snapped from its hiding place and continued to grow as the situation became more serious. Don could tell by her reaction she approved of its size because she raised her eyebrows and grinned in a provocative way. He need not brag, because he felt he was well provided in his penis size, especially with the girth. The women he had been with said they were pleased and that was enough for him.

On the other side of the ledger, Don took in Autumn's sex. Well trimmed and not overly hairy, he could see moisture between her lips as she bent to pull her bikini bottom off. She was very excited and this excited Don even more and his cock took another stride to rigidity. Another example of her excitement came in the form of hardened nipples extending from her close to perfect breasts. They were so well rounded and not overly large. His best guess was that she was a b-cup, perhaps as big as a c-cup, and they looked very natural. It was obvious that she felt comfortable with her nudity because there were no tan lines that he noticed anywhere on her body. Perhaps she used a tanning bed like Don did, although there was a modest color difference where his swim trunks had covered him up. It was hard to maintain an even tan in this type of climate, unless he went nude around the clock.

"Don," Autumn declared, "I have seen many lifeguards in my line of work, and well I might embarrass you, but you have the sexiest body I have ever seen. Believe I am not just saying that. I can't believe I just said that."

"Ummm," Don stuttered briefly, "I am not sure what to say about that, except that it it is one of the nicest compliments I have ever been given. So let me return the favor. As you can see by my excitement I find you attractive as well. As most men would in the position I am in."

"Thank you," Autumn responded.

"I am done young lady," Don returned.

"Oh, I am sorry, go on with your sweet words then."

"I do believe I will," Don leaned forward and added, "before pillow boy starts up again." She giggled and snorted loudly, drawing the eyes of the others in the class, including Sam who smiled at the two of them in his guru best. She quickly covered her mouth, stifling her chuckling and letting Don continue. " Well I was about to say how sexy you were, but after that snort, I am not so sure now."

"Hey," Autumn exclaimed punching Don softly on his bare chest. He smiled broadly, and he could see she thought his remark was funny too.

"Okay ladies and gentleman," Sam announced, "let us continue with our next phase. I would like the ladies to use both pillows. One on the back of their heads for comfort and the other under their lower back as they lay out in a missionary sexual position. For those of you that don't know the missionary position, the lady is on her back with her legs spread enough to accommodate the position of their partner in between. Yes, I know. You all know that, but I don't want to embarrass anyone who might not. Sorry, I didn't want to exclude the male couple, sorry fellas. You might find it a little harder than the heterosexual couples. No pun intended."

The class laughed at Sam's bad attempt at humor. The gay couple giggled the heartiest, which in turn made everyone laugh more. Sam whistled between his fingers to draw back the attention to business at hand. Once the laughter died done, he proceeded.

"Anyway, ladies and my one good male friend, please get into position now. Guys, your job is a much harder, oops here I go again, but I think you will enjoy it very much. I need you to get in between your partner's legs and please void touching her or him. Place your hands wherever it feels comfortable at the sides of their body. Try not to let your dangling sex meet with theirs. Use your feet and or knees to set up your position. You are to lean into it, but again, please do not touch her or him. I am going to let you gain your balance before I proceed."

Autumn watched Don's rippling muscled chest and stomach hover over hers. His cock mere inches away from her pussy, and his hardness was not making it even easier for him to get into a comfortable position. She pulled her legs further apart and he smiled his thanks as he found a better spot to keep still in. The dampness between her legs and the night air made her crave Don even more. He was a chiseled fictional character from a romance novel she might have read when she was in college. It was too good to be true that a man such as him could be interested in her. She knew that her womanly ways could sway a guy, but this was beyond the type of guy she usually caught in her net. As beautiful and confident as she might seem to be, she was far more reserved in her life. To make the attempt to lasso Don, she did something she normally would never do, and that was to go after the man instead of the other way around. To see his satisfied reaction now between his legs towards her made Autumn quiver for him even more.

It took every ounce of his being to not just plow into her glistening tunnel. Don could smell her sex, and it was as alluring as the perfume she wore. He very much wanted to be away from this class and just have his way with her. To taste her, to feel her, to be one with her. His cock was growing to a pre-sexual hardness he hadn't had since he was teenager. As he placed his hands at the sides of her flat tummy, he raised his hindquarters so as to allow his cock to hang just above her most sacred of areas. Sam swung on by and whispered to Don to move his chest closer to hers by sliding his arms up closer and away from the sides of her chest. It was a little difficult to do and maintain his no touch zone required for this exercise below their waists. He did gain control and managed what Sam had instructed.

"Good everyone," Sam cheered. "Now I want each and everyone to take a deep breath in through your nose and hold it for a moment and then a long exhale outward through your mouth. I want you to close your eyes now and do it, but listen for your partner and try to follow each other as you inhale and exhale. Try to breathe as one. In through your nose, deeply now, and hold it for a moment then release the air through your mouth. Feel your partner's breath as they exhale. Listen to them and breathe deeply with them. Be as one. Again and again. Listen and feel your partner breathe. Your breathe, your bodies and soon your minds will be one. Now open your eyes but continue to breathe deeply.

"Now as you breathe, the mate on top will begin to simulate a sex thrust using the muscles of his body. You will push inward as you breathe in and you pull back as you exhale, holding a moment in between. Please keep this rhythm and remember to exhale guys. Start now."

Don found it an awkward task at first, trying to keep from touching Autumn with the tip of his hard cock as well his other parts of his body, and at the same time do the breathing task. He thought it should be easy to do, but lost focus in the eyes of the beautiful woman beneath him. Autumn's mouth was slightly open and the intense sexual look in her eyes had him mesmerized as he swung his hips down just short of her pussy. He also brought his mouth close to hers, feeling her breath and reminding him that he had indeed held his breath despite himself. Before he could correct himself, Sam reminded the group that some of them were holding in their breaths. Autumn smiled as Don let out his air.

"I want you to imagine that there is actual penetration now. That you and your partner are sharing each other's warmth. Focus on what you know, on what you remember from your past experiences. Let your memories flow from the passion you have had. The feeling you get from the interlocking of your bodies, the pure sexual arousal that overtakes you as you meet. Feel it, absorb it all. Everything you know, everything you know as good comes flooding back to you now. Imagine those feelings now."

Autumn heard the words, and they were working on her as Don moved above her naked torso. She imagined his hard cock pulsating as it drove into her damp pussy. Hugging her slick walls as it went deeper with each thrust. This vision held true with her as if it was happening as she felt her hips gyrate on their own accord. The need to be fucked remained, but the illusion she created triggered intense waves of pleasure from the unlocked memories of her best lovemaking. She saw Don as an equal lover, whether it be true or not, she indeed made it so. Every time she felt his hot breath on hers, she felt his lips caress her mouth. Every time he descended, she felt his hard muscles press against her own. She imagined her legs wrapped around his waist as he drove deeper and deeper into her. She felt her pussy walls contract against his warm pleasurable extension. She so wanted it to be true, she willed it to be.

His desire was heightened by what Sam was saying to them. There was a sense of truth in his description. He did draw upon memories as he moved over Autumn. He imagined how warm her body felt locked against hers. He drew a mental picture of how good of her lover she might be. He thought about her movements in rhythm with his. One of things about sex he loved the most were the signs of pleasure manifesting themselves as they became one. On top of his list were the moans associated with the building desire. He thought about how sexy Autumn's voice would be when placed into such a position of passion. He lived to hear her guttural sounds as he fucked her sexy body. He yearned to look into those blue eyes and see the rise of an orgasm he so much wanted to give her. He snapped back to reality when he felt his cock tip braise Autumn's slick pussy lips.

There was a pleasurable shiver elicited from the accidental contact throughout Autumn's body. She felt partially responsible because she was bucking her hips in rhythm to Don's movements. As simple as the glancing touch was, it left a residual need for more. Autumn looked up at Don and saw the same unquenched arousal, and the desire to be somewhere else at that moment was the thought forefront in her mind. There was no doubt, she didn't want to be at the no-touch tantra class anymore.

Don found it increasingly difficult to restrain from simply dipping his penis into her ever so inviting pussy. The contact he had made left him wanton. There wasn't any use in imagining he could continue these movements without the need for more "accidental" grazing. The look Autumn had just given him held the same belief. She too felt the space close between them. She too looked as if she wanted him to do more than what Sam was asking. As if to test this thought, Don made a concerted effort to let his shaft fall between her oily lips. As he did this, she closed her eyes for a second and her mouth gasped her approval. For that one brief moment Don felt the tiniest of pleasure waves course through him. His own orifice leaked a similar fluid mirroring her state of heightened arousal.

"You will find yourself," Sam continued, "at a point where you will want to do more than you are doing. If that is the case, then you have done well. You might also have made contact with each other and now the eroticism is at a level that you no longer want to hold back. The holding back is the Tantra. The tantric exercise is to bring about pleasure deep within you that will be both elongated and different than you have ever experienced before. Don't doubt you can stop yourselves right now. I have seen some of you at that edge of no turning back, but it isn't the wrong path. It is actually the right one. The one you want, and I am sure need more right now than at most times of your sexual life. This tantric exercise is to bring you to a point of arousal that you can no longer hold back. It is what I call the teasing exercise. You can halt this exercise and pull apart from each other now.

"So here you are now, aroused and tempted. Most of you I might add, were not doing very well with your breathing exercises. You need to rely on each other for this. It is essential if you wish to explore what tantric pleasure has to offer. What does it have to offer? Imagine having that feeling right before orgasm, and returning to it over and over again. That would be impressive, right?" Don stared directly into Autumn's eyes. They had actually veered away only for a brief moment since their bodies had parted. She held his gaze and in their nudity, it was evident that none of their pleasure had dissipated. They listened to Sam, and heard most of his words. Yes, the art of Tantra seemed for the most part a worthwhile endeavor. How could it not, when the principle idea behind it was pleasure extended beyond normal means. It was tough to rationalize in their heated condition. Sex was animalistic in its raw form and Don wanted to attack Autumn in his beast-like best, without having to hold back anything. He understood what Sam was explaining to them, but there was one problem with this. His time was limited. He had to be back to work not long after the class was over. There would be no time for long extended sexual exploits using some wild Zen logic of the Kama Sutra. He couldn't wait for tomorrow, and he couldn't wait much longer now. He saw this in the way Autumn looked at him. She knew it too.

"...of course the option was yours. You all chose to be naked here today as most of you feel comfortable with your nakedness. The option is always left with you. Tantra can be a choice you make in time. I have a shop on the lower level of the hospice wing. Feel free to come down and purchase my books..."

With a determination that would be better described as sexually deprived, Don took Autumn into his arms and started to kiss her mouth with all the passion he could express. He didn't care who stared, he didn't care who commented, and he didn't care how disruptive they were to Sam's erotic class of Tantra. The no touch zone was over as far as he was concerned.

It was as if Autumn completely melted into his arms as soon as he embraced her. The touch of his lips brought a tremor of delightfulness to her eagerly aroused body. She exchanged tongues and moved her mouth with his. She was lost in the smooch, and as his strong arms and chest drew her closer, her arms moved along his warm perspiration-soaked back. She always loved the sweat glistened men with the rippling muscles and carved features. She ached to be fucked by him this minute, and she didn't give two cents who was around to see it. As if sensing her disposition, he pulled her up and in one motion, sweep her off her feet and carried her effortlessly away to parts unknown as their kissing continued.

Chapter 4

"Sorry," Don apologized, "if I ruined your tantra experience." Their nude forms moved along the beach, and even though their nakedness was odd, it wasn't rare to be found this way on Eden's private beachfront. They paid no attention to the stares or murmurs from the onlookers. Don was heading to an area that would be somewhat secluded at the very least. An area that couples often frequented for all sorts of private affairs. Don had been there twice with other women, but not for what was intended now. "Don't be sorry Don," Autumn responded, "I always wanted a guy to sweep me off my feet." They chuckled briefly before Don became serious again and buried his face on the nape of her neck. It sent chills all over her body, forcing the slightest of moans to escape her mouth. She loved the sensitive area Don was now taking an interest in. His soft lips caressed her neck with the subtlety of a professional with a degree in the erotic arts. His teeth grazed her skin and left no marks as his lips covered the same territory with massaging qualities.

They walked upwards and away from the lifeguard protected beachfront. Don navigated through some rocky terrain without the slightest problem. When the area flattened out, Don made his way to a white stone path that left the beach into a tropical region filled with green brush and plant life. It was lit by some bamboo posts that had lanterns dangling from their tops. With the sun an hour or two away from setting, the sunlight only illuminated their pathway so much, and the makeshift torches did the rest. Don stopped his kissing for the moment, as he entered the flora and avoided straying from the path as he went forward.

Autumn didn't dare ask Don where they were headed, because if he wanted to, he would have told her. No sense in ruining a surprise he wanted to spring upon her. She was quite comfortable in his grip and he only had to reposition himself once and that was when he was navigating the stones earlier. She admired at the ease in which he carried her, especially as the path rose to a sloping angle. It was such a romantic gesture she swooned at the thought it gave her. After a few minutes of climbing the stones, Don motioned towards the opening up ahead. There Autumn saw only the darkening blue and purplish skies ahead.

When the path ended, the area opened back up to another sandy, rock strewn territory, but they were no longer at a beach. There was a cliff up ahead about 100 feet away that stretched for quite a distance. There were other couples here and there laying close by the edge. There were some picnickers, a few couples embraced, and a handful just sightseeing. There was only one other couple that they could see as stone cold naked as they were.

Don walked to an open area a little away from the others, and carried Autumn to the edge. She gasped at what she saw as Don laid her softly down onto the sandy terrain. Below the purplish and red haze of the clouds and the sun sinking behind them, was the picture perfect blue-green water that surrounded the island. She could see down the depth of the ocean and see the many shapes of coral beneath it. It was a heavenly sight to behold. It was breathtaking, but as she turned to look at her company, Autumn's breath was taking away once more. She felt so lucky to share such a picturesque setting with Don, that there wouldn't be anything she wouldn't do for him sexually at that moment if he desired.

Pulling her left foot to his bare chest, Don massaged her heel and up to and in between each toe tenderly with his fingers. She arched her back as he kneaded the muscles which brought her a wonderful relaxing sensation. He took hold of Autumn's right foot and repeated the same deep massage, until she was laying on her back totally relaxed. He moved down her leg, pulling and pushing at her shapely, muscled calves. Then to her knee and finally her strong thigh. He came within inches of touching her mound before pulling away and down her other leg. Despite all the teasing they had just gone through, he still took it upon himself to torture the horny woman. Without a word of caution, Autumn pulled free of his massaging digits and pushed him until he was flat on his back.

With a shocked look on his face at the sudden change of attitude, Autumn got into position and straddled him. With her ass resting against his stiff cock, her legs parted on each side of him, and with her hands holding his chest down, he made no attempt to lodge her from him.

"You wanted to tempt me some more, didn't you?" Autumn accused.

"Well the thought did cross my mind, I have to admit," Don replied with a huge dimple-framed grin.

"I thought so," Autumn said. She moved her ass slightly against his cock, making sure he felt all of his staff against her. He let out a small groan of approval. "I guess you liked that."

"Now look who is teasing," Don chided. She did it again to him and he enjoyed the tease she was giving him, but he was not going to let it continue for much longer. He was becoming as hard as he was before on the beach, and deliverance was at hand.

"You want more of that don't you?"

"And so do you my dear," Don answered matter-of-factly. With a simple twist of the hips and the agility of a man half his size, he switched positions once again with her. His cock, found her the entrance of her pussy, and as he did earlier at the class, he let the length of his penis slide along the lips of her wet slit. He felt her shutter underneath him, and as he did it again, she let out a soft moan to his delight.

"Oh God, fuck me Don, please fuck me," Autumn pleaded. She ground her hips against him, letting him know her intent was as good as her word. He pushed the tip of his cock into the mouth of her pussy, and it almost pulled him in with the slightest of contractions. He held his ground though and pulled out his shiny member and rubbed it over her sensitive clit. She felt the sudden rise of an orgasm all ready, and despite her better intentions, tried to hold it in like a tantra exercise. She didn't want to cum just yet.

"You are a such a beautiful woman Autumn," Don praised. "I wouldn't want you to do something you might regret later." All along he tempted her with the tip of his stiff cock. He moved the tip it into her again and over her clit, until she squirmed with pleasure.

"Fuck me Don, please," Autumn urged. The teasing was paying its toll, and whether she could hold out became irrelevant because as soon as he started to suck her nipples, she came. She held onto the back of Don's head as he sucked hard against her chest. The decadent cascading waves raced through her body as the orgasm brought about a pleasureful experience. Don didn't want Autumn to let her pleasure halt, so he pushed his cock into her as the last of the waves started to subside. The rhythm was slow and controlled as he had mastered over the years. He kissed her softly as she moaned her satisfaction to him. As he moved, he felt her hips meet him on every thrust into her. Don felt her tight walls squeeze against his sensitive head bringing him his own taste of paradise. She felt so good to him, he barely remembered anything more exciting in his whole life. He felt he was sharing something so special with Autumn that he was taken aback by the flood of emotion rising in his chest. There was definitely a feeling he had he had never felt before with any woman. He wasn't the type that ever believed in love at first sight, but as he kissed her, he kissed her as more than a lover would.

Responding to his kisses, were something more than special because he didn't care to just get off and be done with it. There was so much tenderness to it, that she felt love for the man fucking her just then. She kissed him back with the same fervor as he met her with. She wanted to please him, and doing so she felt the rise of another orgasm within her. She wrapped her legs around his waist and pulled him closer and urged the fucking to move at a more rapid pace. She wanted him to cum with her this time.

Her lips and tongue danced with Don's. His hips pushed into her as he felt her legs surround him. There was too much happening for him to last too long, and as much as he wanted to fuck this beautiful woman to the sun rose anew, he had to end it soon. He quickened his pace, and grunted a bit as the sensations took him by storm. He was close to cumming, and she was urging him on to do so. She bucked against him, riding him from below, their naked forms co-existing as one. He felt the rise mere seconds away, and her moans told him she would do the same as well.

"Cum for me Don," Autumn begged, moving her body in ways that milked his cock so he couldn't resist the oncoming explosion.

"Yes baby," Don groaned. With a few last shoves, they both came hard against their glistening bodies. They fucked like rabbits, riding out each and every spike of pleasure. With no more left to give, they stopped, breathing hard against each other. They kissed some more to let the other know how much they appreciated them at that moment. Don and Autumn felt there would be more. There was plenty of time for that, and as Autumn followed Don back to his room where she would help him change for work, she made one comment they both laughed heartedly at.

"I just want to apologize Don, I forgot," Autumn announced.

"Sorry for what?" Don asked.

"I forgot to breath."

The End

Also by this Author

From the Author

Check my page on Amazon for Updates and interesting info.

Author Central - http://www.amazon.com/Dingus-Guy/e/B00A471T6S
Author Blog - http://dingus-guy.awesomeauthors.org/

If you enjoyed any of my books then please share the love and click like on my books in Amazon.

If you write me a review and send me an email I will send you a free book, or many.
(Just know that these emails are filtered by my publisher.)

Good news is always welcome.

One Last Thing, For Kindle Readers...

When you turn the page, Kindle will give you the opportunity to rate this book and share your thoughts on Facebook and Twitter. If you enjoyed my writings, would you please take a few seconds to let your friends know about it? Because... when they enjoy they will be grateful to you and so will I.

Thank You!

Dingus Guy
dingus_guy@awesomeauthors.org

About the Author

As an author I have dabbled in erotic tales of fiction with stories that you can feel for the main characters as if they were yourselves. My love of hypnosis and the art in which Stephen King made you feel his stories even when you did not want to visualize them is how I approach my tales.

If you can get lost in anyway in the words I say, and they get into your mind, I have you and will make you feel you are in the moment. This is a form of being hypnotized much like driving in a car and daydreaming and suddenly you have passed your exit. Except here, the daydream can make you turned on. You can get much of this in my Chocoholic's Dreams short story. A must read for anyone who loves chocolate.

Besides writing erotic fiction and creating hypnosis videos, I also love spicy food and sports, especially my Brooklyn Nets, NY Mets and Minnesota Vikings. I am active member of the local Minnesota Vikings' Fan Club.

Although I have my kinky creative side, I am a gentle person who loves to help people and make them smile. It is the pleasure I give to others through my writing that ultimately satisfies me the most.

You may also like the books by these authors:

JUST PLAIN BOB

Hazardous Wives

HOT EROTICA
BECOMING A SHARED WIFE, VOL. 2

What happened was my own fault, so I guess I can't cry too loud. But Adrianne gets a little bit of the blame – she didn't have to do what she did. It all happened because I'm a basically insecure guy where my wife is concerned. Adrianne is drop dead gorgeous and had every guy in town hot after her ass from the age of fourteen on. I, on the other hand, was the type of nerd who never even could get a date until I hit the eleventh grade. How I ended up with Adrianne, I'll never know; but I was constantly afraid that other guys would try and take her away from me and that someday she might just realize she had made a mistake and let one of them do it. Add to that, a generally suspicious nature and an active imagination and you had the recipe for disaster.

***

Adrianne and I had been married just a little over three years and up until a month ago I didn't have any reason to believe that she was untrue to me. But all of a sudden, things just started to seem different, you know? I couldn't tell exactly what it was, but it seemed as if Adrianne's body was sending out signals that said, "I'm fucking around." Nothing obvious, nothing that I could see, hear, taste, or touch, just a feeling. So I set out to find out one way or another.

She went out one night a week with her girlfriends and I was out two nights a week bowling. We had a lot of friends who came over to our house a lot, especially on the nights I was out, so those were the times I would have to concentrate on to find out what she was doing. For four weeks I followed her every night she went out with the girls, but all they ever did was meet at someone's place and drink beer and shoot the shit. Once, they went to an Avon party. But none of those nights did I ever see any guys around.

At the same time I was checking on Adrianne's nights out, I was also keeping a close eye on the people that hung out around our house. Most of them were Adrianne's friend and some of them I didn't very much like. I figured if she was doing anything it was probably with one of them. I told the guys on the teams I bowled on that I had some personal problems that needed looking after and told them I would have to sit out for maybe a month. Next, I hit the liquor store and stocked up on what we usually had in the house and stashed it under a tarp in the garage and waited.

The first opportunity came the very first week that I followed her on her girls' night out. It was the next night, which was usually my bowling night, and I had driven a couple of blocks away and then come back to the house. I had already fixed the blinds on every window in the house so I could see in from outside and I got into position and watched. The usual crowd of about eight or ten were there and nothing at all had happened by ten o'clock at which time people started leaving.

Pretty soon the crowd had dwindled to four people and Adrianne - Doug, his wife Mary, Gregg and Tom. I saw Mary slip into the bedroom with Gregg and I saw Doug watch them go. I'd heard that Doug and Mary had an "open marriage" but I had never known for sure. I moved to the bedroom window and looked in to see Mary sucking Gregg's cock, but it wasn't Mary that I was interested in.

If you enjoyed this sample then look for **Hazardous Wives**.

Nicki Homewood
The Debtors' Performance
Exhibitionist Erotica

I sat at the table and prayed for a number higher than eight. The dice felt warm in my sweaty hand and I could feel my heart pounding in my chest. They rolled round inside my hand and I scattered them down the table, closing my eyes at the final moment of ejection as they made their way down the table and settled.

I let my head fall backwards, tried to relax my neck, feeling my rich golden hair fall down my back, hoping against hope that finally my luck had changed. I heard the girl next to me gasp and I tried to determine what that meant for me. Had I won at last?

Three and Two.

Not enough, not nearly enough.

What would happen next, I wondered. I was so far beyond the limit of credit that I had initially agreed that I could not believe they would let me borrow more. My credit cards were already maxed out and however good a customer I was, I couldn't believe that they would let me keep on playing. I had already had an interview with Mr Abadlioi last week after the previous set of losses.

I looked down at the beautiful blue satin dress that I was wearing. I had picked it out because the last time I had worn it, I had been lucky, had come away better than level. I loved the big slit down the front, the way that it showed off so much of my cleavage. Around the casino there were certain rules of behaviour that I loved. Guys could admire a beautiful woman and women could be admired, but no one would make much of a move, no one would hassle you. It was nice, and safe.

Economically it was not safe, I reflected. Economically it was a disaster, a life-changing, misery-inducing, marriage-destroying disaster.

I could feel my string pulling into my ass a little, the tops of my stockings on my hips, the lace gently hugging me to keep themselves in place. The satin was smooth and sexy against my skin and I thought that I may never be able to afford to buy such a garment again.

Silence descended over the table as behind me I could hear a group of people approaching me. I turned slowly with a forced smile on my lips.

"Mrs DiAngelo, perhaps I could suggest that you come this way," Mr Abadlioi asked, a cold politeness still evident in his voice.

Behind him were two guys, not goons exactly but big guys that could look after themselves in a fight I was sure. Not that fighting was exactly my thing.

We walked away from the table and I could feel the eyes of all the people on the floor track me as I walked out past the tables, past the fruit machines and down a darker corridor leading to the backrooms where the reality of casino debts started to encroach on real life. No longer here were you just dealing in coloured plastic chips, this was where cheques and credit cards lived, and debt collectors and lawyers I supposed.

The guys on either side of me didn't even look at me. Here I was wearing a practically skin tight satin dress, pulled tight over my tits, accentuating my 34B breasts that were otherwise unencumbered with cover or support. I knew that men found this dress very sexy. I had seen the looks of lust, of desire in their eyes many times. I knew that my husband loved to see me in it, loved to see the way it showed the lines of my firm breasts, and just gave away a little of my nipples as they pressed into the fabric.

I was shown once again into his office and sat down opposite him, ensconced behind his huge solid oak desk. He smiled at me graciously.

"Well, Mrs DiAngelo, we seem to find ourselves here again. Well, well, well. And so soon," he started.

"I seem to be going through a very unlucky run," I mumbled nervously.

"Yes, well that is certainly clear. But the problem for me is now really just how we are going to recover the funds. I seem to remember last time that you were very keen to keep it between the two of us. Does that remain the case?" he asked, his eyes roaming down over my form.

If you enjoyed this sample then look for **The Debtor's Performance.**

Wives
Lend A
HOT EROTICA
Hand

by **LEON RANDALL**

This was a unique occasion in my 56 year life. I was completely naked with a rampant hard-on in the company of my darling wife (who, of course, had seen my extended appendage a million times before) but also in the company of another couple, for whom seeing my erection was a first-time experience. As a group we were transitioning from being just friends to friends plus 'more'. Russell and I were sitting on the sofa in Jan's and my house, a couple of feet apart, each with our hands tucked at our sides so we couldn't touch our dicks. That was the deal we'd agreed to. We were being watched by our wives who were sitting on the ends of the sofa, enjoying our 'situation'. An hour before, this would have been embarrassingly unthinkable. But now, each of us had our Willies about as engorged and scarlet-purple as it's possible to be, both of us were hard and oozing precum and, at least in my case, throbbing and close to a hair trigger which any moment was threatening to see me tip over that edge and come messily all over myself, hands-free and without even being touched. Sound impossible? I would have thought so, too, until that Saturday afternoon.

* * *

We met Eva and Russell via a nudist website. If you've read some of our other stories you'll know how Jan and I fumbled our way into nudism. I won't go into all that again here, but the highly summarised version is that when our son moved out of the house to live-in at university we suddenly found ourselves able to be all frisky again in ways that you really can't be when your kids live at home. I'm pleased to say that Jan and I genuinely still love each other - are still 'in love' might be a nice way to put it - and are enjoying a revitalised sex life with this newly-found empty-nest freedom. To our mutual surprise and enjoyment we have learned a new thing or two about each other's sexual desires as a result (amazing that after years of marriage that can happen, but it can) and discovered we shared some interests in exhibitionism and voyeurism. We'd led an enjoyable but pretty tame sex life until recently so this opened up exciting possibilities - at least in theory. We were both timid about turning those thoughts into reality. We're both possessive of each other and didn't want new and naughty sexual 'fun' to turn out to be not fun at all and leave us jealous or unhappy that we'd gone too far, too fast. In that context, swinging has a tantalising appeal in theory but we agreed neither of us really wanted that so we looked for softer options. We put our toe in the nudism water as a fairly obvious early step. It promised to be a bit naughty but not likely to get us arrested or divorced. And by its nature (no pun intended) it promised to provide chances to see and be seen. We had aspirations for 'more' than just that, but wanted to take it slowly. So, that's how we met with Eva and Russell.

If you enjoyed this sample then look for <u>Wives Lend A Hand</u>.

A Compilation of Love Stories

Love
and
Lust
Erotic Romance

Amy Redek

With our meal over, she said, "This is my bed," pointing to the large palm leaves that I'd already noted, "and you'll have to sleep on the sand tonight. We'll get some more palm leaves tomorrow for you." So with that, she pulled the unburnt wood from the fire and went and settled herself down on the palm leaves, pointing to the sand next to her. So that's where I went and lay down, seeing her settle herself in the dim moonlight before we said our goodnights to each other.

She at least was wearing some sort of clothing whereas I was only wearing my shorts and I woke up sometime during the night feeling quite cold, and I must have rolled over to her to share some of her body heat, for I was cuddled up to her when I awoke in the morning. She must have known this but never said a word as I rolled away from her and got up and walked out onto the beach to see that my boat was still there. I even went and had a swim and on coming back to the shelter, saw that she had set out two small palm leaves that took the place of plates and on each, was a variety of fruit which appeared to be our breakfast.

With that finished, she wanted to show me over the island but I insisted that we salvaged as much as we could from the boat before it disappeared. And so that's how we spent my first full day on the island, by getting everything that I could off the boat. Lunch had just been nuts and fruit but for dinner, we toasted some spam to eat and she didn't really like the fact that I would only open up one can of tinned peaches. Taking it in turns to spoon out a segment to eat and then shared the juice to drink. She thought it was delicious and wished that I would open another but I stood by what I had said from the start that we would be parsimonious with the tinned food to make it last as long as possible.

What with spending the whole day ferrying this from the boat via the sail, we forgot about getting some large palm leaves for my bed and so, like the night before, I was to sleep on the sand again next to her. But like the night before, I was cuddled up to her like two spoons in a drawer, my body up tight to hers with an arm over her and I know damn well that she felt me when I woke up, for I had a massive morning erection and it was pressed up to her backside. I rolled away from her and went straight down to the sea and dived in to let the coolness of the sea to shrink my erection back down to its normal size.

Yet again, she never said a word but it showed when she said that before we tried to salvage more from the boat that we got some big palm leaves for my bed. I'm sure my face went red at her saying this but this is what we did after our breakfast. I am not going to keep repeating myself but breakfast consisted of the same fare every morning, so take it as read as to what we ate having already said what it consisted of.

So with my bed in place next to hers, we went swimming again to get the last of what could be transferred ashore. This was done by the end of the morning, and the afternoon was spent in building up a fire beacon that could be lit on seeing any vessel in sight. The extra advantage was the fact that I still had the Very Light and flares to send up if needed.

Now for dinner, we had plates to eat from and not palm leaves and the tinned chicken stew went down a treat as did the tinned fruit for dessert. The cheese, what I had left over, had now gone so mouldy as to be inedible and she was going to throw it into the sea but I stopped her as it would make good bait, for I had salvage my fishing gear which later came in full use for catching fish to cook and eat. I think I'm dragging this out a bit being somewhat reluctant to say what happened that night, but I suppose I'll have to.

We still had moonlight when we laid down on our palm leaves, me now having a T shirt to wear and not feeling the cold air so much. But it was her that rolled over to me this night and cuddled up to me and had her hand come over my waist. Now just with having her bring her body up to mine set my own body into a state of flux. With me feeling her breasts being up close to my back and her hand over my hip, aroused me, and my body gave out a shiver when her hand felt the front of my shorts. She felt what was there inside, a man's penis at a full erection and knew exactly what to do with it.

Her hand then moved and slowly undid each button on the front and with the front now being open, her hand went inside and…

If you enjoyed this sample then look for **Love And Lust**.

All Night
Arcade

Jack Ryder

I have always enjoyed working at the arcade. Sort of a playground for adults so to speak. My wife Dana has never been real thrilled with my choice of employment. Especially since I work the night shift and don't get home till well after sunrise most mornings. Sometimes, not till after the lunch time hour.

I chose the night shift because you get much more "action" after dark! Usually a good mixed crowd of curious experimenters thrown together with a group of "here to play all night" folks. I usually do my best to see to it that the curiosity seekers have a good experience so they will want to return again...and again.

Sunday is the only day I have off. I would work that too if I were single, but the wife would cut my nuts off if I did not at least stay home ONE night each week. I have always found that each night has its own type of crowd. Monday is the lonely wife crowd. Tuesday and Thursday are the nights that are the slowest. But I fill that idle time by allowing the street girls to hang out and do what they do.

Friday and Saturday are the busiest nights and they keep me entertained best of all. Although the street girls do have a way of keeping me occupied on Tuesdays and Thursdays. But Wednesday night is what I have always called the mystery night. I am always busy but I just never know what is going to happen next or what kind of group will show up. It is sort of a "pot luck" crowd. And THAT can be very interesting!

Tonight was a typical Tuesday evening. I got most of my evening duties completed between 7 and 9pm as I normally do. During this time frame there is usually a slow shuffle of men that go back to the private booths to suck some cock through the glory holes. These are the wanna-be sort of men that are thrilled with the anonymity of having sex with other men without risking being seen by anyone else. Or having to admit to themselves that this thrills them so much.

It was just after nine when I saw her come into the front foyer leading into the main room. There are three separate areas in the arcade.

The main room is the center part. It is where my customer counter is located. It is where the rows and rows of DVD racks are, the rows and rows of sexy apparel and the glass display counters with all the adult sex toys. There are four hidden cameras that cover the main area. The video screen is behind the counter where I can keep an eye on everything. I was watching her from all four angles as she slowly made her way towards me at the counter. She was gorgeous!

"My name's Dixie, Hun!" She was bent over the counter before I could stick out a hand to greet her properly. Her fluffy collared jacket fell open enough to expose her bare breasts to me. My eyes were riveted to her tits as she continued to look down into the glass like she was looking at the dildos in the case. "I'm new here and the other girls said you are nice to us working gals." Her eyes moved upward to catch me staring at her lovely 36CC globes.

Dixie placed her elbows on the glass but did not adjust her jacket or try to stand up. Her tits were nearly right in my face. "You gunna be nice to me, darlin?" She had a gleam in her eye as she said it and a subtle little grin. "I could be...so nice to you!" She reached over and laid her hand on my arm. "Do you get a break around this joint?" she whispered as she stood up but leather coat wide open. "Somewhere private...where we could...enjoy ourselves?"

Dixie pulled her jacket closed as we heard the doorbell dingle to announce the arrival of two younger men. They took a quick look at her but then hurried to the booths on the eastside of the building. Dixie was smiling sweetly as I dialed my cell phone. "George...can you...cover for me about an hour!" She was now petting my arm softly as I glanced down at her gorgeous shapely legs. The indecently short mini skirt barely covered her honey pot and her thighs looked yummy.

I sat down on the couch across from my desk as she opened her jacket and let it fall to the floor. "So, Dixie...what did you have in mind?" I teased her as I kicked off my shoes.

"I intend to rock your world!" she said it softly as she unzipped her skirt and let it fall to her ankles. Dixie was now standing in front of me in only her garter belt, black sheer stockings and stiletto heels. "That way you will always be willing to have me back!" She stepped right in front of me and I was looking straight up into her dripping wet gash.

"Oh, Dixie, look at that!" I whispered as I reached up to run a finger up her slit.

If you enjoyed this sample then look for **All Night Arcade.**

www.ingramcontent.com/pod-product-compliance
Lightning Source LLC
Chambersburg PA
CBHW061454170626
46811CB00004B/1510